The Foreplay of Providence

The Foreplay of Providence

Ad Infinitum & In Dire Straits

SUSHMITA DAS

PARTRIDGE
A Penguin Random House Company

ISBN: Softcover 978-1-4828-3420-8
eBook 978-1-4828-3419-2

To order additional copies of this book, contact
Partridge India
000 800 10062 62
orders.india@partridgepublishing.com

www.partridgepublishing.com/india

Dedicated to

that Force which is behind everything;

&

the two most beautiful people I had the fortune to be born to Mom, Manjula Datta and Dad, Subir Kr. Datta, the reason of my very existence, whose unconditional love and patience made me what I am today, who believed in me even when I went wrong.

&

my mom—in-law, Kasturi Das and father-in-law Rajendra Narayan Das, who have been a guiding star for me when I stepped into an entirely new world.

Reconnaissance

Thanksgiving is the most difficult job as you tend to miss out people. But my circle is too well-defined to miss anyone.

To start off how can I forget my editor, Mr. Jagdev whose inspiration and comment gave me the courage to pursue my dream . . . "Your expression has the tone and tenor of freedom and joy. It has the sound of the first breath one takes after being under water a few unwanted seconds. Keep it up. You surely must think of publication. Let the world see and experience your passion."

A bundle of talents, Nikkie Gargi, with her magical touch of brush and pen has given a new perception to my creation.

My gorgeous sis, Madhumita and my bro-in-law, Siddhant who have stood by me as a rock in times of despair.

My support system, the most genuine people, my dearest friends, whose encouragement and care has helped me to smile, for being the silver lining,for being the bridge over troubled waters.

A bunch of kids who call themselves 'Bandish' who has so many times brought back smile to my pursed lips and glitter to my tearful eyes with their music.

My loving students who have made me what I am today and for being my inspiration.

Last but not least my world, my husband, Simanta who has been my strength and has stood with me through all the strife and my son, Gaurav, my pride and solace, whose coming to our world gave me a different dimension.

Thank you all for making me what I am today and for believing in me . . . you all mean everything to me.

"Ad Infinitum"

Chapter 1

Everything happens for a reason.

Sometimes people come into our lives and we know right away that they were meant to be there; they serve some sort of purpose, teach us a lesson or help us to realize who we actually are or who we aspire to become. We never know who these people are; they may be our neighbour, a long lost friend or a complete stranger who when we lock eyes with them, we feel that very moment that they will affect our lives in some profound way. The people we meet affect our lives and they are the ones who actually create us and are probably the most important ones.

How true was it for those two people! Kashish and Rajesh, inseparable and bonded by the divine grace. Who else but me knew them better ? From a tender age, I knew them when Kashish and I were just kids, and Rajesh a tad elder to us.

Our world was the three of us, Kashish, Rajesh and myself, the closest of friends, sharing every little thing with each other; the daily chores, our tears and laughter, our fantasies, fights, games and last but not least the pranks and partners in crime. I had always been their shadow, the connector, the mediator, their heart and soul.

But we soon became victim of circumstances. We were distanced from each other just after our teens, razed from our roots for years. Kashish to the south, Rajesh to the west and me hanging midway, maybe to keep a track on my besties from a distance. Though miles apart yet we all were there in every moment we lived. Our parting vows echoed in our minds . . .

In the corner of our lips,
We'll be there in our smiles.
In every dream our eyes see,
We'll be there to fulfil.
In every tear,
We'll be there to share the pain.

With the rise in the odometer, Rajesh turned into a hardcore professional in the corporate world. His professional commitments alienated him from Kashish. Though the feel was always too strong, yet he didn't even know the changes Kashish had undergone nor her whereabouts. I was the pivot maintaining the balance, so I was in constant touch with both my friends with my own capacity.

I had seen Kashish through her smiles and tears, her pathos and misery. She had undergone a lot of tribulations at different stages of her life. Out of pain many a times she had decided to put an end to her life. It was me who stood by her as a rock to counsel her.

Pain was her constant companion and all I knew was that I had to save my friend, release her from the clutches of her agony and make her live. I realized one thing that the panacea of all her agony was her reunion with Rajesh (which she had always craved for). No one else but Rajesh could bring her back that smile, I longed to see in my friend. I had to do something.

* * *

Chapter 2

Kashish, as the name suggests was an artist's delight, a cause for envy and a reason of pride for many. Even at the very tender age she was God's creation at its best. She was a symbol of beauty with brains, grace, subtlety and sensuality.

She was slender as a lily, pink, rosy lips with her hair rippling and shining like a cascade of brown waters caressing her sensuous back. Though an owner's pride yet she hardly could be owned.

Rajesh too was so enticing even at the tender age. There was something alluring in him that captivated the opposite sex. No wonder he was adored by so many, but worshipped and loved only by Kashish, but discreetly. Tall, a few inches over six feet, slender but not lanky. Eyes of deep black, tinged with the sadness of having witnessed too much of the world. His voice, a hypnotic, deep baritone was sensuous with a cut glass English accent. But those weren't the things Kashish had fallen in love with. it was something else, something gentle beneath that hard edge that had always attracted Kashish.

He was always different, to reach him was difficult, to connect to him was far more difficult; when, how and why he would react was beyond one's comprehension. In short he was whimsical, unpredictable, unfathomable. There was always that 'no entry' board dangling in front of his onlookers. But things were different for Kashish and me. We could reach him easily without any inhibitions, maybe that's the true gift of childhood bondage.

* * *

Chapter 3

All these years Kashish had been combating her pain and her soul was frustrated, desolate and deprived without Rajesh who didn't even have the slightest knowledge of it. Kashish, unlike me, was an introvert and would never let out her feelings easily. She would suffer within herself but not share her pain.

Providence played a nasty trick
To abandon her in every possible way
She felt the bruises of her soul
That often forced her to curse her fate
The grief wrecked the passions of her heart

Her wounded spirit imprisoned in the dark dungeon
Suffered as a falcon in its cage flutters,
When it sees the birds soar in the firmament.

Kashish had been griefstriken all these years, her soul battered by the bruises of her unfulfilled dreams; scorn and blasphemy acted like fire upon her heart; humiliation and fear enshrouded her soul; she often felt the pathos of her long lost days, all she could do was to resign to her fate. She cried all alone hoping for a wonder to happen to her.

Long were the days of pain she's spent within her shell.
Long were the nights of loneliness that strangled her to death.
Too many fragments strewed on the streets
She failed to withdraw from them without a burden of ache.
The downs burdened her to make her stoop
The silver lining submerged in some unfathomed sea.
The strength and confidence deserted her
Groveled in the ground she, tormented and shattered.
The memories that once brought smile to her pursed lips

The eyes that saw the beauty of the trees and moonlight.
The ears that heard the sweetest melodies
Converted into a horrifying flame searing the heart.

However hard she tried to satisfy her own people she failed. Whatever she did was subjected to ridicule. Desperate and desolate many a times she tried to commit suicide but providence had something else in store for her. Kashish cried and sulked failing to find an escape route. Her looks and body betrayed her too. The agony showed itself on her and made her lose her kashish.

It was her beauty that had once forced her parents to christen her as 'Kashish' or attraction, but it was all gone. Circumstances made her lose everything, destiny touched her with its icy cold hands. One fine morning she got herself lost in oblivion. Noone knew where she was.

As said, that when one loses something one realizes its worth. That's exactly what happened with her people. Her absence reminded them how valuable Kashish was. But there was no looking back for Kashish. She had reached a point of no return. All she knew was that she was alone in this cruel world and she had to fight her own battle. The only person she could revert to was me. I was the only witness to her every drop of tear. Then I made her realize that she had to rediscover herself and mend everything that had gone wrong with her, a complete transformation was what she needed.

* * *

Chapter 4

What could be better than running away from the maddening crowd to Mussorie? Yes, that's the place which had always attracted Kashish. It had a lot of fond memories tagged with it, memories that she would carry to her grave. Where else could she go to find solace?? No one knew her there. She was a complete stranger and she preferred that way. All she needed was to redefine herself.

The young woman she was,
Weathered through many a winding depression
In search of the unfathomed seas
Disheartened, turned into a calm lake

Solitude n yearnings turmoiled her heart
Like the mad elements of the sky.
Looked up she like the begging petals
For that one drop of dew
Old memories flashed like passing shadows
When evolved she like a thought
Sparked to life like a gust of wind
Breaking the fetters of agony
Emerged she the enticing enigma.

I recorded every change of hers as she had none but me to resort to. It was past three years and Kashish was the phoenix reborn from her own ashes.

There stood She reborn and free.
Like the dying flower coming to life by the first drop of dew
Like the young man's anxious heart enlivened by the tender touch of love
Like the soldier freed from the grip of his long exile
Like the carefree child prancing in the heart of nature
Like the flock of birds soaring in the blue sky

Like the fragrance of wine hovering in space
As birds in the enchanted forest . . .
There She once more like a phoenix touched the sky,
To rise from its ashes.

* * *

Chapter 5

Kashish was a child then when she had first met her prince charming, yet the first glance of Rajesh was so enticing that she could never flush those memories out of her system. She knew at once that she had met the other half of her soul. He was the one who deserved her heart and nothing would work out with anyone else.

It is as people say, that first love can never be forgotten and it was love at first sight for Kashish. She would not miss a single occasion to meet Rajesh and when she met it was like being on cloud nine for her. But Rajesh had never taken her seriously though she was very dear to him. She was quite aware of that, yet could not control her emotions. Her people barred her from their union yet she would break all fetters to be with her prince. The child in her soon turned an adolescent and the platonic love gave way to passion. Days rolled, years passed yet Rajesh failed to understand her love for him, or rather he denied it. Maybe for him, Kashish was just a kid, not attractive enough to arouse attraction in a young man.

But for Kashish, Rajesh was the last word. She had grown up with this fantasy—

Your eyes shine upon me like the shining stars
Those lips that I yearn to kiss are delicately made
If wood be strong then your body is better done
If hair be silk then black silk grows on your head
I have seen bold, handsome n magnetic men
But have never imagined such wonder as in you
Each time you step into my den
You open to me a new path to wander
I love to hear you speak, and well I know,
This music can't have more pleasing sound
I claim I never saw a God go
But you when come, brings all peace to my mind
So by heaven I know my love is rare and beyond compare.

This was her dream, her Rajesh! She had worshipped him in the deep dungeon of her heart without expression. But her prayers were neither heard by God nor her human-god. She had to surrender to her fate and lead her own life completely oblivious of Rajesh.

* * *

Chapter 6

Tidings of Rajesh did reach her through me but Kashish never delved into it. "Live and let live" was what she had always practised and believed in reciprocation on being reciprocated. She paved her own path so did Rajesh, their childhood path forked into two, thus were they separated.

Kashish's fight for survival continued, her endeavour to transform herself was in full swing. Changes were rampantly visible. It took three long years for her to emerge as a diva !

Kashish was reborn but old memories still haunted her, wherever she went her eyes hovered for that one glance of her human-god. Who knew when, where and how would she meet him !

Yes, I made it happen for Kashish. I had to make her come out of the trauma to live once more, be happy and smile that enchanting smile for which many hearts swayed.

* * *

Chapter 7

It was an early spring evening when Kashish very unwillingly accepted an invitation for a party. Who else would have sent her the invitation but me? But she couldn't even comprehend it in her wildest dreams.

Though not in the right frame of mind, yet she accepted the invitation. Who could deny the call of destiny? Wrapping herself in her red chiffon with a halter sleeve gold blouse with a deep neckline revealing her sumptuous cleavage, hair rippling down to her hips, with a big black bindi and her danglers, she stepped into the party. Her very presence created an inexorable silence as eyes dazzled and gaped at her. Kashish felt a sudden discomfort but yet managed to keep her cool. She seated herself in an extreme corner and me at the farthest opposite corner, a vantage point from where I could observe all her moves.

The bewildering crisscross of colourful light rays and moving shadows created magic around her. She sat and waited for her friend to come. But she never turned up! Instead the waiter with an ingratiating smile on his false face pampered her by offering a glass of French wine.

Far away seated at the bar counter was an irresistible hunk sipping his drink and hovering his eyes over Kashish with much discreet(the other one who received the same sort of invitation).

Kashish was every man's challenge to own and a tease to every man's manhood. So was this hunk, he was no exception. Challenged by her oozing sensuality, he approached in slow footsteps towards Kashish.

'Good evening Maam.' 'I am Rajesh', 'Would you mind having a dance with me?' Kashish looked up unsettled by this sudden overture of friendship but soon regained her composure. 'My pleasure', she smiled (memories flashed upon her inward eye suddenly as she saw her human-god !). Rajesh, not recognizing his childhood bestie, yet in love at first sight, soon held her soft, manicured hand. The very warmth of her touch unstabled him, yet he led her to the dance floor. As they stepped onto the dance floor the music caught them by surprise. 'The Lady In Red'. They couldn't stop giggling, and that instantly bridged the gap between them. The ice broke and Kashish was all in her swings and swirls. Her grace left Rajesh awestruck. It seemed he was cast under a magic spell charmed by her beauty. It was irresistible, his heart thumped and yearned to touch every part of her body. His first move was on that streak of her hair that had been distracting her for quite sometime. Rajesh touched the streak and his fingers had the first feel of her soft skin. He held her a tad tightly without any resistance. It seemed Kashish too had melted by his strong gentleness. His left hand held her slender waist and soon they reveled in their comfort zone. They moved closer to each other feeling the warmth of their breath. Rajesh made the second move. His lips tasted the sweet wine of her lips. It was like the passionate foreplay of the serpents that followed in their mouths. Captivated by her touches Rajesh dragged Kashish out of the dance floor. She followed him (as always) just as a child follows its mother blindly towards an unknown destination. Me, the silent onlooker enjoying every move of theirs !

The car door opened and they both flung themselves into the backseat. The door slammed and closed. Inside was chilled with the full blast of the AC. The music was on—'Can you feel my love tonight'. The stage was all set. In a split second, Kashish enchanted by this godly demeanour in front of her was lost completely. It was not for the physical attraction but more for the love in her heart that Kashish gave in spontaneously.

The drapes of her red chiffon slipped off her shoulder unknowingly revealing her enticing cleavage. Rajesh could do nothing but gape at them. He deftly maneuvered around her stone hard breasts till he devoured them fully. Kashish trembled under his magical touches. Bending down, she Kissed him gently. Rajesh moaned with this move. His hands ran through her brown cascade and then with a sudden jerk he tightened his fist and pulled her nearer. The wildest kiss followed, both melting in each other. In one breathtakingly swift move Rajesh undressed her. The perfectly chiselled body of Kashish was a delight to watch and a challenge to Rajesh. He was quick in flaunting his manhood. The fire ignited in Kashish while she remained speechless. He pulled her so that they could consummate their desire. Kashish groaned, closing her eyes as she reveled in the sensation. Like the feats of a magician Rajesh grabbed her and twirled her so as to pull the rein himself. Their trembling bodies accelerated to find release. 'Oh I Love U', murmured Kashish's frenzied voice. In ecstasy, Rajesh could hardly hear what Kashish had just pronounced. As Kashish continued her teasing they became all sensation and all consuming again. The overflow of passion raised them to the heights of frenzy. They lay unshrouded not touching, not holding but just staring at each other and admiring.

Rajesh looked down at Kashish brimming with ecstasy and whispering, 'I want you now, I want you always and forever'. 'You are mine' and once again the two bodies clung to each other. Foolishly enough, Kashish thought they would never be separated! But as said, man proposes god disposes.

* * *

Chapter 8

As Kashish returned to the party after her rendezvous, her eyes had the treat, her body graced by the touches she had been longing for. She had waited all these years for that one glance and that one touch.

But what about Rajesh ? Did he have the same feel ? I doubt ! He could not even recognize his long lost mate. Though Kashish could read this yet it hardly made any difference to her. She was with her prince, her soulmate after decades. She had awaited this moment for years, how could she deny such a chance !

How ravishing she looked with that twinkle in her eyes and the blush on her cheeks ! That magical touch did it all. It's then I came to the forefront to meet my bestie. She couldn't believe her eyes but yes, she knew me so well that she at once realized the reason of her coincidental meet with Rajesh. She knew it was me who had served her prince on a silver platter garnished with a tad of mischief.

Kashish's sojourn soon came to an end and she had to return to her quotidian struggle for existence. As she left, I could see the deep pain mingled with a sense of fulfillment in her beautiful dark eyes. But how long would she be able to fight this pain? I regretted. I wanted to make her happy but her separation from her prince once again brought more pain and tears to her. It made me skeptical thinking whether she would withstand her agony.

* * *

Chapter 9

Rajesh too was back to his den after that party, trying to meet the demands of his work. But something did trouble him. There was a fatal sense of isolation creeping into his mental soundness; some strange pull which distracted and defocused him. This incomprehensible reason unsettled him 24x7.

One evening I suddenly received a call from him. I instantly knew the reason as he never used to call up on week days. He was normally so preoccupied with his work that he hardly got time to socialize. His work was the mantra of his life and he would not compromise on that ground. When I received his call, his grave voice resounded of unspoken pain.

It stirred up my curiosity to fathom his discomfort but I waited for him to unveil it.

After about an hour of conversation where I had been a passive listener, he suddenly enquired about Kashish. All these years he was completely oblivious of her. I was stunned by this sudden enquiry. What made him think of her? Did he recognize Kashish at the party? My heart skipped a beat, but I was soon assured that he could not associate that 'lady in red' at the party with his long lost friend, Kashish. From his conversation it was evident that it certainly stirred up his emotions; memories and sensation played the role of temptation and his constant desire reminded him of his friend. He started probing into the matter and wanted to find her.

Rajesh urged me to reveal where she was. But how could I forget my promise to Kashish? So I had to avoid his volly of questions with great difficulty. I somehow managed to divert the topic. Rajesh expressed his deep desire to be in touch with Kashish. He confessed that life had changed dramatically after that party. My heart pounced realising that he could not get over the kashish of Kashish (his lady in red).

* * *

Chapter 10

Meanwhile, Kashish on her return was equally heart broken. When you are around someone for a long time they become a part of you and when they change or go away, you fail to know who you are without them. That's what Kashish was suffering from. She became completely unaware of her existence, her return from that party made her lifeless as she failed to overcome the separation. She was shocked that her Rajesh had failed to recognise her. But that's how things were. Men forget everything when it comes to work; and when it's a workaholic like Rajesh, what more could one expect?

People say time is the best healer but was it applicable for Kashish? She was slowly sinking, traumatized, depressed and desolate.

Clutched in the jaws of Melancholy,
Wounded by the agony of Solitude
Imprisoned in the darkness of disillusion,
There waited She.

Nights after nights she would lay awake gazing into the wilderness trying to seek answers for her unquenched questions, nobody realized when she had sunk into a depression. She refused any intake of food; no sedative could comfort her. Soon she was clasped by the sharp jaws of death after all hopes had died. She was then removed to the hospital, sad but true! Kashish was admitted in the special ward where trauma patients were treated.

* * *

Chapter 11

Since I got no message from Kashish for a long time I became restless and anxious. She had never done this before, whatever may the reason be, she had always intimated me. Unable to hold back my anxiety, I straightaway boarded the train for Mussorie. As I approached her door, my heart leaped in terror. Her domestic help came to me to break the horrifying news. I was shocked. Wasting no time I ran to fetch a cab to go to the hospital.

I rushed to the reception counter and enquired about Kashish. Soon I was ushered to the Intensive Care Unit. My feet trembled as they stepped forward, weird thoughts clouded my mind, my heart skipped beats in utter terror as to what awaited me. I was numbed with fear. Soon the door opened and the gush of wind with the smell of medicine hit my olfactory receptors giving me a nauseating feel. I stood still at the door shocked to see Kashish all in tubes from the artificial respirator. But gathering all my wits I rose to the occasion and moved towards her.

Family isn't always blood. It's the people in your life who want you in theirs; the ones who accept you for who you are. The ones who would do anything to see you smile and who loves you no matter what.

It's said that even in the most critical or unconscious state one can identify one's closest bondage. So did Kashish. My presence in the room was immediately felt by her and with a lot of discomfort she managed to open her eyes. Though she had a blurred image of me yet a smile lit up her pursed lips, tears welled up in her eyes and she started to sob.

The whole ambience resounded with the intense pain that had thrust Kashish into this state. I could not bear it any longer. I broke down completely. It was unbearable for me to see my bestie in such a state. She tried to utter a lot of things but failed miserably. All I could hear was a groaning sound.

The attendant prevented me to stay any further as it was making her restless. So I turned and followed the attendant out of the room. I was baffled, my senses had paralysed, a sudden mental block struck me. I felt helpless, I didnt know how to react. I thumped myself on a nearby chair. I felt completely lost in a no man's land. The only thing that echoed in my ears was that familiar name of Rajesh, fingers instantly hovered over the keys of the cell. The waiting seemed decades!

Senses soon dawned upon me that I was not supposed to reveal Kashish's identity. What would I do? I could not have handled this critical situation alone, I needed Rajesh to stand by me. An idea struck me. Why not pronounce that a close friend of mine was critical? By this I would avoid his queries then and my work would also be done. I decided on this and waited for him to take the call.

Finally my call was answered."Rajesh, I need your help, a very dear friend of mine is in critical condition, I need you." This was all I could utter before I choked. He went on asking me questions which I couldnot answer. I handed over the phone to the receptionist for Rajesh to get all information, (cautioning her not to utter the patient's name). The sweet soul he was, immediately ensured, "Dont worry dear, I will be there by the next flight." His comforting words made me regain my strength.

Rajesh had always been my comforter. There was nothing that we did not share. Even in his busy schedule he would cater to all my needs. A friend like him is nothing but God's blessings, standing by in times of distress; understanding me even better than I myself did. He was a friend, guide and philosopher to me. I could not do anything without him, my strongest support system, the most genuine person, my dearest friend, whose encouragement and care had helped me to smile always, for being the silver lining and the bridge over troubled waters; for bringing back the smile to my pursed lips and glitter to my tearful eyes. Who else could I think of in this hour of distress? That's what true friendship is all about.

* * *

Chapter 12

When I sat in the waiting lounge monitoring the proceedings, I was transported to those good old childhood days, reminded of the happy times when Rajesh used to come and pick us up from school. We would walk through the lanes and bylanes of the City of Joy prancing carelessly and carefree, indulging in all sorts of childish pranks having no worries and tension of life. How we used to play mischief with the roadside hawkers, satisfy our tastebuds with all the objectionable street food ('phuchka' as we called it). How happy we were those days when we trodded down the lanes singing and dancing in joy; when life taught us in small little ways to be happy with simple delights. We would run after the butterflies, catch them, touch their wings and then let them go; collect flowers from gardens, sneak into people's houses, climb the mango trees and pluck mangoes till the caretakers would drive us out; dance in the rain, gather hailstones and the list goes on. Everything came back to me at that moment, I could smell the fresh fragrance of those exhilarating times we three shared.

Gone were those days of smiles and tears, fights and love. How I wished god could grant us one more childhood to relive those moments !

* * *

Chapter 13

I was suddenly stirred up from my dream by the nurse who frantically came looking for me. The sight shuddered me since I could smell something wrong. The nurse hurried me to Kashish's room and from the door I could hear the frantic and desperate yells of my friend. I lost all strength to enter, but I was somewhat pushed by some unseen force, maybe because I was needed to be beside my companion. Kashish was in acute pain! The pills she had consumed in her depression had started their action. She tried to throw up but failed. The burning sensation made her scream. The doctors surrounded her, preparing to remove her to the operation theatre for an intervention of gastric lavage. The spasms made her crumble and crawl. As I went near to comfort her, Kashish held my hand and cried out "Rajesh". That was enough indication for me to realise what she wanted. We could read our minds so well that even a glance or gestures were enough for us to understand each other. Holding her hand tightly, I nodded to reassure her. I knew she was certain that her end was near. The overdose of powerful tranquiliser, she had thought would put her to eternal sleep and release her of the pain forever, but the reaction was so very different. Her stomach churned in intervals with the stabbing pain, the burning feel finally making her lose consciousness. The doctors hurried her out of the room to carry her to the operation theatre. She had actually attempted suicide in her depression ! The dose of tranquiliser could not take her life but was enough to damage her whole system.

* * *

Chapter 14

Pangs of solitude engulfed me as I stood all alone in the room combating with my fear of losing my friend; apprehensions creeping in whether I would see her back alive. Tears rolled down and I had a collapsing feel. The knock at the door got me back to my senses. I saw Kashish's maid standing at the door. She approached me and handed over a few chits of paper which she had discovered under the pillow of Kashish. Jitters ran down my veins as I knew these chits would unfold her misery. Flipping through them quickly, I could hardly stop myself from breaking down as they unlocked the door to her agony.

"The pangs of loneliness still turmoils my heart. The poison of the sting rises up my blood with every thought. Darkness enshrouds my world, agony pierces my heart. I open my tear-kissed eyes everytime and I hear a rustling of wind, hopeful to see the approach of my love. But in vain. I curl back into the world of pain without the least chance of a glimpse of my love". The lines ached me to see her suffering.

I continued to read her heart, that revealed her fantasy.

"Dawn appeared and silence roared with the passing of wind heralding the surge of ecstasy in me as I sit with glazed eyes looking down at my Adam lying beside me. His irresistible sweet fragrance mesmerising me, trembling every cell of my body. I feel the exhilerating outburst of ecstasy oozing out of every pore climaxing me to frenzy. The warmth of my body awakens him and he gazes upto me with his thirsty lips yearning to quench his thirst sipping into my lips. His long artistic hands slowly approaching to caress my hair touching my lips with his magic and strong gentleness. I close my eyes as if to relive my dream world with my man feeling an invisible pair of wings carrying me to the heights of ecstasy. His face brightens with my warmth and me blushing with his touches melting like the snow-capped mountain by the first adoration of the sun. Wrapped in each other's arms we taste the overflowing wine in our lips. Our naked bodies touching each other at every point diffusing the heat and burning us in our passion till the wait is no longer awaited. The dormant volcano that lay years in silence turmoils for the outburst as he slowly delves deep into the well of blazing lava. The trembling bodies accelerating to find their release. The erruption follows the rhythm of the hearts as we both get lost in the spontaneous overflow of emotions heightening to release the long awaited rapture."

I remembered how Kashish had always expressed her passion about the hills. How she had yearned to be in the laps of the snow-capped mountains as she always had a strange connect with it. Her feel she had so passionately depicted in the next lines.

"Avoiding the clamour of the throngs I moved along knowing not my destination. Like a child following his mother I followed my love, forgetting my very existence, staring at his beauty. My eyes blinded under his spell ascending and descending painfully on the twisting rocky path till I experienced the magnificient mystery of existence amidst the intoxicating call of the hills. The hypnotic beauty of the snow-capped mountains embraced by the open arms of the blue-throated sky captured my fancy. The sweet fragrance and the chill in the air left me awestruck. I was like the free bird hovering in the spacious firmament. Along with my love I stepped into my paradise intoxicated by his magical touches. Embracing my body he bestowed a dizzying kiss on my trembling lips. It was paradise on earth carousing with the elixir of my life !"

Reading through the lines all I could feel was the intense plight my friend had suffered all these times being alienated from Rajesh.

Could I blame Rajesh for this? The question haunted me every moment. Whose fault was it? I started believing in destiny. What is destined to happen will inevitably happen, I had always strongly believed in it. That one force above us may it be Krishna, Durga, Christ or Allah or in any other form will give and make us do exactly what He wants. Today I see it with my own eyes. Everything is preordained, our share of suffering or happiness. I started believing in the previous birth and karma.

How true they seemed to me, else would a simply adorable person like Kashish ever suffer? Yes, that's the reason Kashish was in such misery, completely disillusioned and desolate.

* * *

Chapter 15

Rajesh was winding up his work and rescheduling his itinerary. His flight tickets were lying on his table. He was busy but completely preoccupied, every moment my words haunted him. He tried to decipher who that close friend of mine was. The dilemma caught on him and it affected his smart modus operandi. He grew impatient and just could not wait to reach me.

As expected I received a call. The anxious voice of Rajesh sounded very perturbed and inquisitive."I am reaching you in another four hours, hope everything is fine there,"he said. I decided not to bother him much, so avoided the details of Kashish's critical state. Before he could further probe into the matter to satisfy his curiosity, I snapped the conversation. I had to divert the topic somehow and I did it by showering a few compliments on him which he was really worthy of to retain my promise. He informed that he was rushing for the airport so we decided to hang up but promised to be on text.

I desperately wanted his support and courage to pull me through this crisis. How could I forget his concern for me whenever I needed it? He was a true friend indeed.

Whenever I think of Rajesh I am reminded that when we honestly ask ourselves which person in our lives means the most, we often find that it is those who, instead of giving advice, solutions or cures have chosen rather to share our pain and touch our wounds with a warm and tender hand. The friend who can be silent with us in a moment of grief and bereavement, who can tolerate not knowing, not curing, not healing, but face with us the reality of our powerlessness, that is a friend who cares. Rajesh was tailor made as per these words. He was the kindest soul I had ever come across.

* * *

Chapter 16

Though I was surrounded by hundreds of pale visages gaping at each other, awaiting anxiously for their dear ones at the hospital lounge, yet I felt myself completely deserted. Uncanny thoughts clouded my mind and I was caught amidst a whirlpool of fears making me jittery. Every minute seemed an hour and it became horribly painful to live those moments.

Looking into their blank faces I could well feel their trauma as I myself was stuck up in the similar situation. Each time a nurse or a doctor passed by, my heart beat faster, apprehensive of some bad news. Human beings are so negative on facing a crisis; this had always been my case. I could manage my own problems but when it involved my loved ones I was a total failure. I became completely defunct.

It was almost past four hours I was sitting still at one place without a drop of water or a morsel of food. The monotony of this dreadful silence was suddenly broken by a commotion in front of the operation theatre. I jostled my way through the crowd hoping to see Kashish. True it was Kashish, but in greater danger. The doctors accompanying her were looking for me. When I reached, they pronounced the devastating truth. Kashish was certainly not out of crisis though they had pumped her stomach. The overdose of strong tranquilisers had damaged her brain and she was in partial coma; chances of complete recovery could only be a blessing of divinity.

My ears were paralysed at the news, I stood motionless as Kashish was taken back to the ICU. A few doctors attending her were hopeful of her recovery. When I spoke to them they revealed that due to prolonged separation from her beloved, unfulfilment and suppression of desire, she had succumbed to severe depression. Kashish had a severe attack of Dysthymia caused by feeling of hopelessness, worthlessness, insomnia, extreme mental trauma and recurrent suicidal attempt. She could revert to her normalcy only if there was a chance of restoration of her lost bondage, if only her desires were fulfilled.

But how would I do that? The thought perplexed me further. On one hand I had to keep my promise to Kashish and on the other hand I had to save my friend. Destiny played a nasty trick on me. The turmoil was heart—wrenching, but I knew I had to do this unpleasant duty. I looked at my watch, less than an hour left for Rajesh to arrive. What would I tell him?

* * *

Chapter 17

Caught in the worst possible dilemma how to face Rajesh, I saw the door of the lounge open and standing there was none other than my comforter and crutch. Any distress and this man would be there for me; a tinkle and he would cross the mountains and oceans for me to be by my side. And today I needed him the most to save my friend.

I hurried to him and threw myself to cling to him like an infant clinging onto its mother for solace. I cried my heart out and got lost in our own world, not bothering where we were or who all were watching. I knew my strength was there with me and I could fight any battle ! Though ravaged by emotions yet I was cautious not to reveal Kashish's identity.

Atleast I would not do it. Let Rajesh unravel the truth himself.

I ushered him to the ward but Rajesh stopped suddenly. I knew not why. Something must have struck the chords of familiarity for him. Maybe he recognised Kashish or was it his lady in red? He did not speak a word, instead slowly moved towards her.

Kashish was lying dead as a log, completely motionless wrapped in that green cover, tubes all over her body, machines attached to her, monitoring her heart and pulse rate confirming every moment that she was alive. Yes, she was alive, actually she had to be for her Rajesh. How could she leave us?

Rajesh sat down beside her on the stool, gazing at her, trying hard to find some resemblance. Time had come to a halt. Rajesh lifted his hand and touched Kashish's cold body. He turned around to look at me seeking answers for the innumerable questions battling in his mind. I stood unmoved keeping my fingers crossed not to face his sudden unavoidable question. Once again he turned to look at Kashish, grief-striken. He called for me and as I neared him I saw his eyes filled with tears. All he could say was "Why did she have to do this to her?" I had no answer. I did not even understand whom he meant. Did he mean Kashish or his lady in red?

He went on saying "How much I missed her after she parted from the party. I had been frantically looking for her and now finally when I find her she is in such a state." He started to sob. "Oh God! Why did you have to do this to her?" Rajesh could not control his tears and I had never ever seen him so weak, sobbing like a little boy !

I at once knew that he had madly fallen in love with his "lady in red" after the party. I smiled as my game plan was a success, but now what? How do I reunite them? I remembered the doctor's advice. I somehow had to hold back Rajesh till Kashish recovered. To my surprise I did not have to put much effort. "I won't leave her till she recovers" and his words relieved me . . .

* * *

Chapter 18

My responsibility was shared with the presence of Rajesh, so I decided to leave them and take a walk to refresh myself. I came out of the hospital that had been traumatising me for the last couple of days. I had not had anything to eat properly, neither did I sleep. The pressure was too evident on my countenance. I needed a break desperately.

It was dark and cold outside, a damp cutting wind was racing about the roads, only a few street lights showed my way. But where was I heading to? There was no destination for me, it was just an aimless stroll; a futile effort to soothe myself as my mind was too cluttered with the thoughts of Kashish.

The evening turned darker and I felt more and more dejected. So preoccupied was I with my own thoughts that I did not even realise that it was over two hours I had been wandering around. Suddenly I came back to my senses with the ringing of my cell. I guessed it right, Rajesh it was, but instead of any further bad tidings, it made me excited. I literally ran back to the hospital reaching the ward completely exhausted and breathless. I could not have taken time to see what Rajesh had just intimated me. Some slight stirrings, streaks of consciousness and feeble rays of hope were noticed. The doctors were all in action to attend to my friend.

When all roads get blocked we, mere humans resort to that one force and I was no exception. I could not see what the doctors were doing to Kashish to bring her back to normalcy. So panic—striken was I that I came out of the room and started my prayers. I had always believed that if you put your heart and soul in your prayers that force above responds. I had my earlier testimonies, one just needs patience to forbear.

* * *

Chapter 19

The tussle went on for quite sometime, the doctors desperately trying to revive Kashish from her semi-comatic state. Though she was responding and the doctors were hopeful yet to me everything was in utter darkness. I still could not see any positive sign. That charming smile of hers would only satisfy me. Would I ever see it again? The fear haunted me and was driving me mad.

Sitting right near the head of Kashish's bed was Rajesh. It seemed he was determined not to move away from Kashish or leave her alone. He sat there motionless touching her bed and I knew exactly what he was doing. Whenever he used to be perturbed he would surrender himself to 'The

Destructor' and resort to the chantings of Shiv mantra. That was the apt moment to chant the Mahamrityunjaya mantra. After all he had to save his lady in red.

It was over two hours then that Rajesh had been chanting his mantras without a break, as if in a trance. His face had swollen up, eyes were red, tears rolled down his cheeks. What a sight it was! Even the gods would stir up from their eternal silence and bless such a devotee. The doctors had told that only a miracle could set her right, and there it was! The miracle was in front of our eyes! Kashish opened her eyes, her lips trembled, her fingers shivered and she tried to move. The monitors which had gone hay wild slowly started recording normal readings. She had the first smile on her face after three days since she had been in partial coma. The biggest surprise came to her when she turned her head and saw Rajesh still meditating. Tears kissed her eyes, she wanted to say something but was awestruck at the sight of her human god. She must have felt the divine presence of the lord Himself !

The doctors hurried to sedate her once again restraining her from getting excited which would have further worsened the situation. But how could she sleep? She had to feel the presence of her

Rajesh. She turned to touch his hand and gazed in awe. It was a dream come true for her to see that he was eventually there.

The confusion in the room broke Rajesh's trance. He slowly opened his eyes to witness the wonder he had been waiting for. He couldnot believe his eyes nor his ears when I unveiled the outcome of the miracle. He stood motionless as if he had lost all power. He was completely drained out. I had once heard that people who pray for others in distress take in much of their negatives. I was a witness to it. Rajesh was completely devoid of any strength, almost on the verge of collapsing. I hastened to fetch him some water and help him to sit.

He gazed at me, hundreds of queries in his eyes. His unspoken words conveyed all his thoughts. After he regained stability, I unfolded the proceedings that had taken place a few moments earlier in that very room. Rajesh turned to look at Kashish who by then was fast asleep under the effect of sedation. The calmness and feeling of satisfaction was all over her face, she looked like a princess as if in her world of fantasy. A little smile crossed Rajesh's face and his eyes revealed the joy of winning a lost battle! His happiness knew no bounds realising that his desperate call was finally answered.

Old memories flashed upon my inward eye. The story of Behula and Lakhindar had once left a deep impression in our minds when we three were kids. So many questions had cropped up at that moment. Could anyone love so intensely to snatch the lover from the jaws of death just as Behula had crossed all hurdles along with her dead husband to miraculously get back his life from Yama. We had always doubted such a story. So many times we had also laughed at this story but all my doubts were cleared. Miracle did happen and it happened that day !

* * *

Chapter 20

'It surely calls for a celebration, isn't it?' Rajesh very innocently asked me and I couldn't deny it (as if I had ever denied him earlier). As things were stable we both decided to go out and celebrate Kashish's come back.

There was a cafeteria nearby and we walked down to reach there. Outside the sun had bid adieu. The last flock of birds were chirping their way back. The azure sky was touched with the hues of purple. It was late evening and the roads were already deserted. I searched for a ray of light, but in vain. The cold wind was piercing and we were possibly the only two souls on the road unable to see a step ahead due to the thick fog. Though happy yet there was a peculiar vacuum engulfing us, despite being together, we still were miles apart, abstracted in our own thoughts.

The painful silence was soon broken by the mystifying tunes of the harmonica and I knew instantly from where it came. I turned and saw Rajesh playing, an age old practice of his. A born artist he was, he had magic in his hands. His long artistic fingers used to swirl, swing and flow on the keys of the grand piano. I had always been mesmerized by his artistic raptures and once again was spellbound by those tunes he so often used to play in our childhood.

Yes, those old memories were stark, real and nostalgic! How we scribbled on our backs, chuckled and guffawed, minted nicknames, stole glances at someone who crossed our daydreams. We craved to redeem a hundred of those scintillating moments, thought through the blur of our tears that they were all gone as we had grown up, but that day treasures were still alive in the gallery of our hearts because the best memories do not give in to the press of the delete key but await to flash instantly on our touch screen!

Music for me has always been a mesmerising outburst of ecstasy unravelling absolute bliss, fantasizing a dream world in perfect harmony pacing towards a new horizon. And when it was Rajesh it had a different dimension and feel. I always used to get completely lost in its passion and I had a similar effect then. I reveled in whatever was happening.

How could my friend know that it was just what I was craving for? Maybe that's what friendship is all about. You have a special connect that doesnt need words to convey, it's the feel, the vibe that makes you understand. I presume that was why telepathy always worked between us so well.

Traversing through the deserted roads we finally reached our destination. All we needed was a cup of steaming coffee to pep us up. The ambience was beautiful, the cafeteria encircled by the tall pines with a well-pruned lawn, exotic flowers adorned the garden. The dim lights from the hanging lanterns added to the magic—a place so apt for the lovers. But there we were the two closest souls bound in the chord of friendship, a more intense feel, a much stronger bondage than any lover could possibly share.

We were so spellbound by the enticing beauty of nature that we preferred absolute silence. Not a word, just the type of silence one experiences before a storm. No sooner did the waiter serve our coffee than Rajesh came up with something that unstabled me completely. "Why is it that I feel your friend is none other than my Kashish?" I was completely taken aback. I knew Rajesh had recognised her but I remained mute. I had no answer for him. I desperately wanted to avoid his question, but in vain. "Please dear save me from this turmoil", said Rajesh. I felt his urge to have my confirmation.

"What will I do now? How will I avoid his question? Will it be right on my part to keep him in dark?" I thought. On the other hand I had my word to Kashish. I was in a fix, both were dearer than my life how could I cheat any one of them? I was caught between 'should I' or 'should I not'.

* * *

Chapter 21

At the hospital Kashish had woken up from her deep slumber. She was trying desperately to combat her weakness, to move in her bed but her movements were restricted by the pipes and cables attached to her body. The attendant ran to summon the doctor as Kashish once again became restless, maybe because of the after effects of the strong sedative or did she once again feel deserted without finding Rajesh in her room? She coaxed the nurse to find us. The helpless Kashish was thrust back into her desolate state once more. The doctors panicked as they checked her up and enquired about us immediately.

It was over four hours by then that Rajesh and myself were out at the cafeteria. Rajesh's doubts became stronger gradually. The silence that prevailed upon us was soon broken by the call from the hospital. It agitated Rajesh and he looked at me puzzled. Without a word we left to reach Kashish, not a word was spoken on the way. Somehow we wanted to reach, wish we had wings to fly to her.

Rushing through the door, we could only hear her painful voice calling out for Rajesh. My heart ached to see her helplessness and desperation. I felt the moment nearing when the scrambled bits of the jig-saw puzzle would fall into their right places! Just when Rajesh reached, her voice vibrated in the whole room, "Will you stay with me when I become old?" Rajesh was taken aback. But alas! I stood paralysed seeing Rajesh still unable to put the last piece of the puzzle.

I knew love knows no time, no distance, no bounds, it is eternal, ad infinitum. God willing, who could ever break a bondage? But everything seemed a fallacy then. Though I was the happiest person seeing the two of my best friends clinging to each other and crying like mad kids, yet it was not the way I had wanted it to happen.

"Why did you have to do this, stupid girl?", asked Rajesh. The smile lit up Kashish's face, she once again blushed at his words. "I could not carry the burden any longer without you", Kashish replied. "I needed you every moment but you were not there for me." I could see Rajesh pained on hearing this innocent confession of his lady in red. Whatever Kashish had just pronounced was meant only for her human-god but what was heard by Rajesh were from his lady in red whom he had met at the party. Unfortunately neither god nor her human-god still had mercy !

* * *

Chapter 22

I left the room completely bewildered. How was it possible that Rajesh could still not recognise Kashish? Had Kashish changed so much? "Is physical appearance the only key to identification? Aren't feelings and emotions enough to connect to your loved ones?" I was disillusioned but failed to rise to the occasion. I wanted to run to them and reveal the truth but I was desperately struggling between the promise made and the urge of conscience to break it.

With the hope that another miracle would happen, I waited outside. I left them to solve their own puzzle. It was almost an hour that I was struggling with my own predicament but slowly I lost my patience. I could no longer bear the suspense, so I made my way to the ward once again. What I witnessed was pathetic—Kashish was crying like mad and as she saw me she lost all control. "He asked my name. God how could he?" she cried out.

This innocent query gave her the greatest shock. She started choking and became so restless that the monitors once again recorded abnormal readings. She succumbed to a severe cardiac arrest. I hurried to call the doctor but by then Kashish was sinking.

* * *

Chapter 23

The team of medical assistants barged into the room in no time. The ICU was fully equipped with the latest hi-tech machines to provide all possible medical support. The doctors immediately swung into action by doing the CPR followed by the artificial heart pumping. As I saw this panic-stricken situation, I could well gauge the gravity of Kashish's condition. I realised her end was near and I would soon be losing my friend. This time no miracle would happen, that was the inner call of my intuition.

The doctors were struggling with the artificial heart pump and injecting the LSD. In turns of three they kept on pumping but their efforts were in vain.

It was on the fifth turn that Kashish responded with a yell. The monitors started recording her heart rate but it was so feeble that we all knew it wouldn't sustain for long.

Rajesh stood speechless, petrified at the sight. Another yell and Kashish pronounced "Kashish", followed by that traumatic silence! Something stirred deep in my gut, I could feel something getting stuck into my throat and suffocating me. I ran to her and took her in my arms. "Dont leave my dear, you can't leave us and go Kashish." But no response! I wanted to cry but I choked, maybe because I wasn't ready to accept the heart-rending truth. Kashish had become completely cold by then, nothing could revive her as she was destined to leave.

Hearing me Rajesh fell with a thud helplessly on the ground near us. "Why didn't you tell me before that it's you, Kashish? Why did you do this to me?" He kept on repeating as I sat helpless. I felt I had committed the worst possible sin, but what could I have done? I was bound to my friend. Rajesh gave me a blank look and that terrified me. Would I lose my solace also? He started blaming and cursing himself for not being able to comfort Kashish in her agony.

To err is human but whose fault was this ? It was certainly no human error but the game plan of that Mr. Supreme up there who plays all the tricks. Who can ever deny His moves? That's why till date I am baffled why Kashish had restricted me from revealing her true identity.

Rajesh felt that devastating assault somewhere inside him which made him cry and I saw that Herculean mass crumbling in pain. He continued blaming himself for not recognising his childhood mate at the party, with whom he had grown up. He fell in love with her then at first sight but he was so allured by her sensuality that he failed to get the feel of his soulmate. He began to coerce himself for committing such a sin. That guilty look on his face became unbearable.

I frantically tried to change my expressions but my facial muscles had frozen. I lost all grasp over the situations unfolding before us—mere puppets we were in the clutches of destiny! Powerless to calm Rajesh, I sat completely wrecked holding my friend in my arms. My guilt feeling was killing me. The thought of facing Rajesh later was far more agonising.

The harrowing silence was disrupted by the coming of the ICU in-charge. He came to fetch us to fulfil the hospital formalities.Rajesh left with him but I decided to spent some more time with my friend. I looked at her as I never wanted to take my eyes off her. She still looked so beautiful, though pale, but her big, dark eyes still had that glitter which seemed to speak to me. Blood gushed down my spine and I slowly closed her eyes with my hand putting her to eternal sleep. The last touch I had of my friend!

Chapter 24

It was nearly an hour when Rajesh returned and informed that it would take some more time to discharge the body of Kashish. So we decided to wait in the lounge unable to bear the grievous sight any longer. The door to the balcony was open. We dragged our shaky legs towards the door as we desperately needed some fresh air. It was pitch dark outside, cold and the piercing, chill breeze stirred up our numbed senses. We stood still till the cold wind continued to hit us.

The lounge was comparitively vacant as it was nearing midnight, the noises had faded away giving an eerie feel. Most unexpectedly I heard an approaching footstep. As I turned to see, I realised it was Kashish's maid who had come all the way at that hour of cold weather on hearing the news. In the darkness I couldnot see clearly but could certainly make out that she was holding something. On enquiring she very emphatically said that it was for "Rajeshbabu" (as she knew him that way). I got the hint and therefore didnot persuade her further to hand it over to me.

She must have been strictly instructed by Kashish to give it to Rajesh only. Her behaviour aroused a lot of curiosity in us and we couldn't wait any longer to see the belongings.

It was a gift box beautifully tied with a red ribbon bearing a note "ad infinitum". I could see Rajesh's hands trembling with apprehension and anxiety. I myself was more jittery as I knew this would lead to more of Kashish's anguish. Peeping into it we were in awe—a bunch of letters she had written to Rajesh but never posted.

Underneath the letters was a bracelet Rajesh used to wear—the one which Kashish disliked so much. On one of those evenings when they had discreetly met escaping all eyes, Kashish had told him to remove it. Rajesh like an obedient boy had taken it out and thrown it from the balcony. Who knew that this crazy girl would later go out in the dark to fetch it and preserve it till her last breath?

The last of the contents was a small red box which had the ring bearing Rajesh's name which he had given her as a token of 'ad infinitum' before we three had parted. She had worn it all these years but I suppose had taken it out and kept it in safe custody before leaving for the hospital. A sudden spark of doubt hit me. "Did she know that she was leaving never to return?" The realisation bound us both in excruciating pain.

And then Rajesh did something which he had never done before. He held me tight in his arms and cried, uttering the most devastating words—'If only you both had told me the truth'.

But who can deny the play of Providence? After all Providence has its appointed hour for everything. We cannot command results, we can only strive.

* * *

In Dire Straits

Chapter 1

We all have our days when we feel we can hardly survive. Sometimes our dreams are shattered, friendships fall apart, loved ones hurt us, finances crumble, sickness overtakes us or even lose people whom we love. Under such circumstances most of us are left dejected and we tend to lose faith, blame it on destiny. There are very few who combat with the toughest of times clinging onto hope or rather defy the play of providence. Such are the souls who often leave footprints on the sands of time.

On her fortieth birthday, Smriti looked ravishing and gorgeous in her black tight skirt with a black jacket and high heels. Her black, silky hair flowing down to her slender waist, unkempt by the cool breeze entering through her window overlooking the sea. The moon was almost full spreading her silver sheen over the roaring waves and trespassing into her living room through the open curtains giving a warm touch to her otherwise humble and warm domicile.

The interior of her domicile portrayed a mystic tapestry of marvels with the best collection of antiques and exotic paintings adorning the walls. Her taste for home decor was much in tune with her mien. Smriti loved to decorate her home just as she fancied to adorn herself. In short she was a perfectionist with an artistic bend in regards to decor. She believed in having the best in whatever she possessed and did in spite of her tryst with destiny.

Standing at the window she gazed at the galloping waves. She had just returned from an event. In her hand she held a book that she received as her birthday gift. As she flipped through the pages, tears pooled up in her eyes. The tears were certainly not of sorrow. The roars of the waves mingled with the chimes of the number of windchimes heralded the joy of her victory ! Memories flashed like moving shadows in front of her eyes. Whatever she had done till date had left a mark. They had become memories for her or her people, good or bad.

Smriti or reminiscence as her name suggests had always been a source of recollections. Born in a middle class family, she was always the very pampered one as she was the youngest of the siblings. The pampering she received was not because she was the youngest but it's because of the circumstances under which she was born. Here too she created history and left enough marks in the world of medical science. Her birth was a challenge then for the doctors who were not so well-equipped forty years back. Every single moment and every move was a challenge for the surgeon who operated her mother. The risk was hundred percent—it was fatal both for the mother and the baby. But she denied all obstacles and brought smiles to the family in spite of the harrowing seven hours surgery. The baby had to be rescued from a well of tumors in the mother's womb! Smriti stepped into the mortal world with an external wound. Maybe that was the first indication or challenge of providence that was to unfold in her life. The one-dayer was least concerned forty years back and today too she is least perturbed with any hurdles posed by the trick of destiny.

* * *

Chapter 2

More of a tomboy, Smriti exuded the boyish streak in whatever she did. Indulging herself in the sport that was more mannish, which demanded more physical strength, she evolved carefree as to what people had to remark. Though very masculine in strength yet she was brimming with feminine grace. A rare combo she was, that had many a times put her into the clutches of misconception. But that posed least concern for Smriti. An independent mind like hers would never really indulge in what others felt for her. It was her life and she desired to curb it in her own accord.

The coltish adolescent soon evolved into a symbol of grace and sensuality. Beauty with brains was her typical trait and she proved it in whatever she performed. Her smooth skin, deep, dark eyes and black, silky hair gave her looks that had the touch of class; even though that mane of hers was often cropped, chopped and butchered according to her mood swings. But whatever she did blended so well with her persona. Her characteristics which she had imbibed from her paternal side were reflected both in her looks and demeanor.

Smriti had an undying love for art and literature from her very childhood which she had so carefully nurtured and that disabled her from pursuing any other profession. English literature had always allured her and she fulfilled her desire to master it. Her love for art associated her with glamour and turned her into a hardcore professional in the corporate world connected with style and fashion. This provided her a means of aristocratic living in spite of her prodigal manners. But the hardcore professional also had an instinct to write which she always dreamt to fulfil. Though a pastime affair yet she aspired to leave a mark through her writing.

The blessed advantage Smriti had was she never looked her age or rather she never allowed age to set into her looks. A few layers of fat here and there would often be fought with rigorous exercise and crash diets to keep her in shape. Though a fitness freak, Smriti never compromised on satisfying her taste buds. A connoisseur of good food, she would often be an object of joke among her friends. It was fun to see her devour the last morsel of food. Be it fish or crab, Smriti would leave no bone unravaged. The satisfying look in her eyes would often bring pleasure to the host. The satisfaction would rise to its height if the food was accompanied with French wine served in the finest cut-glass goblets. The food and wine would create a magical trick on her excessively sensitive tongue and the pleasure would reflect on her otherwise glowing visage.

Smriti was a class of her own—a bundle of idiosyncrasies, yet an extremely adorable person. But not everyone could intrude into that zone where love was in abundance. That tender heart was intentionally cocooned inside a hard shell. People often were misled by that but those who knew her well tasted the difference.

* * *

Chapter 3

It was her sixteenth birthday and Smriti had decided that it was time she went on her first date. Calls and messages kept pouring in. Finally getting disgusted, she called up her best friend in whom she had always confided.

Shruti was her childhood friend and Smriti trusted her completely. Shruti had long back had the pleasure of her first date and had flaunted many a times in front of Smriti. But her diverse interest in sports and reading never let Smriti think about romance. For her that was a very girlish affair and she stayed away from it. But the 16th birthday was something special. It brought with it a deviation in her thought process which was otherwise very focused.

"Shruti can we meet up for sometime today?", Smriti very anxiously asked her friend as if in some turmoil.

"Ya, sure, but what's the matter? I know it's your d-day but you always prefer to be with your parents on your birthdays." "But I need to talk to you. Meet me at the cafeteria, please, near your house," said Smriti. At 4pm they both were together and Smriti could not hold back her excitement to reveal the reason of their meeting.

"I am going on my first date finally but I'm not aware of what all you do there," exclaimed Smriti very innocently. This was never her cup of tea, and she never indulged in such silly matters.

Shruti who by then was quite experienced decided to groom her amateur friend and briefed her with important tips. But Smriti had her very strict set of rules and would not deviate from them at any cost.

Finally it was time for Smriti to step into a completely new world, a world she was totally unware of. Though a bit shaky at the initial stages, yet her expertise to handle any situation helped her to conceal her discomfort. Her date was a typical character from Mills and Boon's stories—tall, dark and handsome. Smriti looked cute and beautiful as usual. In a short time, they were comfortable dancing and holding hands. The red roses and the gift did have a magical effect on the adolescent mind but Smriti did everything to hold on to her mindset. The first kiss soon followed. Her hero was all set for further intimacy, when Smriti suddenly requested for a cup of coffee. The chivalrous hero called for the nearby waiter with his audible expletives. But by the time the order was complete and he turned to continue his love talks with Smriti, the girl was gone, gone forever, nowhere to be seen.

Even at a young age Smriti was accomplished with the art of reading through one's mind. That rather indecent gesture to fetch the waiter was enough for Smriti to sum up his character and abandon her first date. Much later Smriti had jokingly confessed to her best friend about that disgusting behaviour of her would have been hero and how she ran out of the cafeteria never to be found again.

Though brought up in a middle class family, yet her upbringing was extremely polished with set precepts and values. Education and respect for others were of prime importance. No compromises were acceptable on these grounds in her family.

She had grown up among the best of etiquettes and decorum. How could she have tolerated such undesirable conduct?

These instilled values and etiquettes had posed a lot of problems later in her journey of life. Her taste was different, her demeanor so very different from her friends. Her friends had often made fun of her—"Smriti, you are so selective, you will have to create a man of your choice to be your life partner." Smriti preferred that way and she had thought she would stick to her thoughts. Who knew what was awaiting her?

* * *

Chapter 4

As she stood near the window, Smriti's attention fell on the pompous marriage procession flaunting on the road below. Memories flashed and she was compelled to contemplate over the dreadful events of the past. It was exactly fifteen years back, circumstantially on a similar day with same situation when she was anxiously awaiting such a procession which she thought would bring her a life time of pleasure and happiness. She remembered everything with utmost distinction. It was the incident that later forced her to lose her reverence for the institution of marriage.

It was the day when the wedding bells rang for her. But hardly did she know what was in store for her. Over the years it brought with it immense mental trauma, humiliation and heartbreak. Her dreams were shattered. The woman who was known to be particularly selective was forced by the play of providence to make a wrong choice. She had no one to turn to as she had denied her parents and had opted for this marriage. Three long years had given her unbearable mental and physical torture, complete detachment from her parents and the loss of her job. Many a times had she decided to renounce her life. But something from within had prevented her to take such a step. A fighter that she was, could hardly resign to the hands of fate.

One night she decided to break all fetters and release herself from that dungeon. She knew the world outside would not be very easy for her. There was no support, no family to stand by her. It would be a strife all alone, all the way. Yet Smriti was all set for it. She left with almost nothing, a meager savings that would not let her survive for long. But she was resolute to make it happen. Her aspiration had to be fulfilled at any cost.

That very night she managed to escape from the clutches of death, because a few more days in that relation, the world would have witnessed the end of her. It was extremely cold that night, the moonlight along with the street lights were mitigated by the thick fog that had set in over the road and sidewalk. Smriti walked hastily through the emptiness trying desperately to avoid the scrutiny of the few curious passersby. Smriti was heart sore and disillusioned unable to decide her destination. The ambience harmonized so well with her present mental state.

Smriti managed to board the first train that she saw at the station. She just had to leave the city which had dispensed so much agony. She felt an immediate discomfort when she discovered that the compartment was almost vacated of its occupants except two men huddling up at one corner. She felt eerie yet had no option but to stay. She could well sense the impending danger but by that time the train was already on the move. In no time the two men attacked Smriti as anticipated and started to molest her.

As self defense Smriti always used to carry a small pen knife, though fragile to look at yet deadly when in use. This was the right moment which demanded its help. Smriti dauntlessly thrust it into one of the men's leg. In a split second the two brutes were shaken by this sudden retaliation. Smriti, capitalizing on that situation ran to the door. By chance she observed the train was interconnected.

It gave her an easy escape route. Smriti managed to reach a compartment that was fully occupied. She fell with a thud and sat down on the floor. It did not really matter where she sat, Smriti just had to be safe and be in the midst of people.

* * *

Chapter 5

Destiny took her to a new world, a completely new place. She had once been there in her childhood but that was under the protection of her parents. Now she stood all alone to combat the befalling challenges. She stepped out of the station apprehensive and perturbed. She neither had a place to go nor a job to sustain her. Yet she was geared up for the struggle.

In the cab she was suddenly reminded of a friend. She immediately called her and to her surprise Smriti had a warm reception. Hearing her condition, her friend gave her asylum. Soon Smriti was in the midst of known faces. Her safety was assured and security guaranteed. She managed to get a job in a well-known company because of her earlier association and experience in the corporate world. Life seemed to begin a smooth sail. She had her own apartment to stay and a secured job to sustain her.

Five years passed without any disruption. Smriti was settled, mentally stable to pursue with her dream along with her work. Her job demanded a lot of socialization thus she became associated with many people, made a number of friends and not to forget the professional foes also. Smile was back on her.

Life is nothing but a roller coaster ride, not a smooth sail on a calm sea. It's only how people face it. Some resign to the hindrances, some put up a strife, some defy and continue. Smriti belonged to the last category and never wanted to resign. The twists and turns in her life could hardly make her resign. She believed and lived in the present. For her, past was dead and future, a mirage which she never wanted to chase. Whatever came on her way she did what was expected of her.

It was on one of those socializing spree when Smriti was invited to a grand party abounding in high profile guests hosted by the top notch of the corporate world. Smriti had always made her presence felt wherever she went with her looks and mien which captivated her onlookers. The evening was magnificent with the most expensive food, drink and esteemed acquaintances. She was completely spellbound by the spectacle and was reveling in the sensational happenings. Smriti was perhaps the only one who did not belong to that class but had gained an entry in lieu of her performance.

At dinner when everyone was busy gulping down the delicious food and pouring out generous words of gratefulness, a sudden sound of gunshot caught them by surprise. Forgetting all norms of civility and formality, people out of panic behaved in the most uncivilized manner. In no time police intervened and started interrogating the panic stricken guests. It was assured that Smriti too would not be spared. Providence once again stung her with its icy fangs. Even though completely oblivious of the cause and outcome of the gunshot, Smriti was victimized and taken into custody. The spectacular evening crashed completely with the attempt to murder the host.

Smriti's innocence was evident yet she was dragged into this chaos. Along with a few more suspects, Smriti too was taken away for further interrogation. The trauma and humiliation that followed was unbearable. Smriti hardly knew anyone who could rescue her. The night in the police custody with flash lights and press releases tarnished her reputation. She realized immediately that her days in that city was over, and she would lose her job.

Though her innocence was beyond doubts yet she was forced to plead guilty. That one night of mental trauma was enough for anyone to lose sanity. But Smriti was so different. Her exceptional ability to curb any situation helped her to free herself from the police custody because of her convincing evidences. But by then she lost everything that she had gained with such difficulty in that city over the years. Her reputation, status, job and friends everything was gone in one blow. She realized at once that the struggle to start from the scratch was on. Her last straw, the friend who had given her refuge few years back in that very city also deserted her.

Smriti had to leave Bangalore the very next day. Once again wounded by the tricks of destiny, she began her journey with whatever belongings she could gather and get herself lost in oblivion. This time things were more difficult for her. Smriti was in no state to face any more hurdle, so she decided to board a bus. She made sure it had enough occupants as she was suddenly reminded of her deadly experience few years earlier.

* * *

Chapter 6

Smriti's exile period in a remote town in the north was traumatic. The unforeseen incident had made her lose her image completely and she had no other option but to seclude herself from the world to avoid humiliation and disgrace. She had to do a few odd jobs to sustain herself, an old couple, kind enough, gave her asylum. She lived in a secluded, single room away from the maddening crowd.

This painful isolation soon became evident on her health, she became feeble, lost her physical strength which she used to boast of earlier. But she did not allow this to rot or decay her mental soundness. She was a fighter and would remain so under any circumstances. Every moment she craved for liberation, to be amidst human voices, clamor of the cities and the glamour of her profession; to have once again the warmth of a beautiful home, revel in the beauty of nature and breathe freely. Somehow she managed to suppress her hankering with the hope of liberating herself one fine day.

I felt my heart thump suddenly,
With a terrible shudder was I awakened
Like the mother woken up
By the scream of her infant
I was lost to see myself desolate
Struggling against the raging elements
Disrupting the silence of existence
I felt myself slipping into the quicksand
Trembling to approach grave
Submerged into obscurity
Let me not immerse into a world
Of Pretention and Falsehood
And leave the world
Like an empty bottle
Discarded by a drunkard.

Smriti dreaded such obscurity. She never wanted to leave the mortal world unnoticed. Her aspirations were different. So she challenged her creative mind to make the difference. "Why not leave footprints through my compositions?" She always used to think. Thus the inception of her innumerable poems began. She wrote not to gain popularity but to retain her sanity and to treasure her natural flair of composing. In her solitude when she wrote, she was at times overcome by the bleak hope that someday, someone might find her creation. Hope is all that we humans have to keep us going!

Slumber groans under the pain of broken wings
Failing to transport me to the world of dreams
The fire goes down and turns into ashes
The light of the lamp dims and disappears
The fierce tempest of loneliness roars
Yet hope and waiting never ceases.

Unlike the earlier incidents, this time her battling spirit was chained down by the painful loneliness and Smriti, many a times desired to relinquish her life. Long were the days of pain, she spent within her shell; long were the nights of loneliness that often strangled her to death. The downs burdened her to make her stoop, the bleak hope got submerged in some unfathomed sea; the strength and confidence abandoned her and she was crushed in the ground shattered and traumatised.

* * *

Chapter 7

Out of desperation when we mortals cry out for help, that force up there, however cruel it may prove at times, does respond to our desperate calls. It programs our life in its own accord and makes us dance helplessly in its tune. We are not even aware of what is in store for us. We act as we are directed. Even in our pain and strife It stands by to witness our capacity to withstand our appointed share of pain.

Smriti's predestined share of pain was about to come to an end as her desperate cries were finally heard. That force had to resign to her beckoning and finally grant her a second chance to rediscover herself.

After five tormenting years of isolation, Smriti happened to come across a stranger one fine day. Though very apprehensive yet Smriti responded to his sudden overture of friendship. Perhaps, Smriti still exuded that attraction which allured the stranger to stop by her and offer help.

The stranger was in the lookout for a dynamic, young, creative mind who could assist him in his venture in the advertising world. Smriti harmonized with his requirements so well that he immediately offered her a job.

Providence had endowed her with unbearable agony but now it was time for gratification. Smriti's obsession to be a part of the City of Dreams was about to be fulfilled. Her new job offered her placement nowhere else but in that dreamland that never sleeps, pulsating, alive and throbbing with life, the city which is the hub of the biggest corporate houses, fashion and glamour. What more she could have expected?

Smriti was simply awed by this sudden twist in her destiny. She was left with no option but to accept the offer. Somehow she needed to be back in that world which had so cruelly ousted her a few years back. There would be no looking back any more. She was hell bent in changing the course of her life.

The god sent stranger had once seen Smriti in Bangalore when she was at her best. Her expertise had often been discussed at the corporate level where she had established herself on her own strength. She was free willed, self-made and on a perpetual high on life. That's what made all the difference. That's what made her an eyesore, often getting trapped in professional rivalry. Dinesh had come in contact with Smriti when she was working for an event for a fashion house. He had seen the relentless effort Smriti had put in and also her smart modus operandi. He was on her lookout from then but her sudden disappearance snapped all source of contact. Dinesh had lost track of her completely, in fact everyone who knew Smriti were in complete dark about her very existence all these years.

Five long years of absolute detachment had made Smriti lose her courage and confidence. She was at her wit's end how to cope up with this new life. She had always longed for challenges. Adventure allured her but now she was scared to face the new challenge. She wondered what would her days be like, what was coming her way in the future?

Smriti had never been bothered about all these before. Maybe age and the burden of misfortune had forcibly altered her thought process. All these years she had always yearned to be out in the world to be free, rejoice in the sunshine and rain but why then was she so worried? She needed the courage and confidence to serve her new company with reliance and show the world that she was still worthy and she had to have the world in her stride once again, she had to prove herself. She fought within herself to regain confidence and trust that spring would come back yet another time.

* * *

Chapter 8

Dinesh was quite worth a second look. He was moderately tall with sharp features, fair and an exceptionally good talker. His sweet talks would win over any heart. He had that striking capability to mesmerize people with his words and smart moves. Smriti had had an opportunity to witness this when she had first seen him in Bangalore. How Dinesh had resolved a fight which otherwise would have resulted in a big commotion.

Dinesh possessed that X-factor needed to make a difference and that had been an advantage for him all the way to build a successful career at such an early stage. Surviving in an ad—world and running a creative agency was no child's play without a godfather and tough competitors. But he had managed a long list of clientele from the top corporate houses and his work spoke volumes about his efficiency. Now that his business had picked up pace and the work load pressing on him, he needed an assistant to shoulder the responsibility.

When he first saw Smriti years back he knew at once that he had got the right person but nothing materialized then. Perhaps, it was not the appointed hour for it to happen. But what is bound to happen will always happen. Destiny brought him back to that remote place in lieu of a shoot for an ad campaign. It was there that Dinesh chanced to have the most unexpected glance of Smriti involved in some odd jobs to earn a living. The sight appalled him as he could not fathom the reason of seeing a successful professional in such an abandoned state.

His curiosity dragged him towards Smriti and that's how he came in contact. Dinesh was determined to find out the cause of Smriti's isolation but she was a hard nut to crack. Not everyone could reach that depth where Smriti had locked up her secrets. But Dinesh was too patient and determined.

Smriti accepted his offer and agreed to move in with Dinesh. Though that option was not very favorable for her as Smriti always wanted her space, yet she had no other choice at that stage. She was almost bankrupt by then and needed a shelter to survive. After all beggars cannot be choosers.

Dinesh gave a warm welcome to Smriti into his small two bedroom apartment. It was a typical, disorganized bachelor's den with things strewn all over. It lacked the warmth of a feminine touch. Smriti was offered the second bedroom which was usually kept locked but occasionally used when Dinesh's mother used to pay him a visit. Smriti lost track from where to start. She needed to settle the apartment to make it livable for her. The kitchen was left completely unused apart from a few cups used for the morning tea. That's all that was prepared there. The waste paper basket abounded in cigarette butts as Dinesh was a chain smoker which was quite repelling for Smriti as she detested smokers. Yet she had no choice but to accept the undesirable situation.

Meanwhile, Dinesh was out of the city for a couple of days. On his return he was completely taken aback to step into a transformed ambience. His apartment was totally done up, it spoke of a home with a woman which he had yearned long since. Soon both were in their comfort zone sharing experiences, laughing at jokes, watching films till midnight over a cup of coffee and enjoying the weekends on the beach. They started enjoying each other's company. The house soon turned into a home with the warmth of friendship.

At workplace the scenario was completely different—two hardcore professionals at their best, arguing and fighting over difference of opinion without any mercy. But it was Dinesh most of the times who had to resign to his very stubborn assistant turned partner. Yet it was a rare combo to watch. In spite of all the fights and disputes there was always a discreet mutual admiration and respect. Work was their obsession and many a times they would sit through the night to achieve success. In tense moments Dinesh would pace up and down in his room with a cigarette clenching and unclenching his hands till he attained some solution. Smriti would silently wait for the barometer to drop and pacify the situation with a cup of black coffee that Dinesh loved. Perfect understanding without intrusion into personal space made them the best of buddies apart from their professional bondage. Soon they were recognized as one of the best creative agency.

Their combined effort got them this status. Smriti was once again back into the corporate scenario in lieu of their clientele and was welcomed back after her painful exile!

* * *

Chapter 9

All this time Smriti never forgot her companion that had kept her mental stability in times of distress—her beautifully done up file where she used to keep her compositions. She pursued with it even when time had changed for her. That was her priceless possession which she didnot want to share with anyone not even with Dinesh.

It was almost a year that Dinesh and Smriti were sharing the same apartment. But Smriti needed her own space, her own home now and wanted to shift. Since she was financially sound by now she could afford her own domicile which she had always aspired for. Thus her hunt for an affordable apartment began. Smriti was always allured by the beauty of the bay so preferred to put up somewhere near the sea.

Her search came to an end when Dinesh, a day before her birthday, took her to a new, beautifully furnished apartment overlooking the sea and held out the keys to her. Her happiness knew no bounds and for the first time that hard nut cracked and Smriti was in Dinesh's arms holding, kissing and hugging him tight. That was her birthday gift from Dinesh! A gift she would cherish the rest of her life.

Life changed completely for Smriti. She had had her share of pain and agony and now it was her time to soar. She turned her apartment into a beautiful home with her warmth and decor. Dinesh was a witness to every change of hers and Smriti was ever indebted to him. He had been her friend in need and her only solace.

Over the years their friendship intensified and became more intimate. After the horrifying experience years back, Smriti was very skeptical in committing herself to anyone. But it was Dinesh's love and understanding that gave her the confidence. She blossomed once more with his touches, regaining her lost glamour and rediscovering herself.

* * *

Chapter 10

Smriti could never forget that party which had brought unbearable pain to her. It often used to haunt her in her sleep; make her restless and yell in fear. She needed to go there once and settle a score with the hostess who had done her wrong. She could not even confide in Dinesh. Although Dinesh had asked several times about her past but Smriti was stubborn not to reveal her secrets. But now she needed his help to free herself of this constant pressure of vengeance. She never thought of harming who had done her wrong but she had to prove her innocence and reveal how craftily she was victimized. The hostess had misjudged her husband's liking for Smriti and so she took her revenge on

Smriti at the right moment. How could Smriti forget such humiliation? It became her nightmare.

It was Friday, and Smriti was in the office planning out for the next venture. The guard came and handed over two invitation cards. Such cards came in numbers into their office but they never used to pay heed to them and were destined to go into the waste paper bins. Smriti and Dinesh were never interested in those parties unless they were very personal.

That day was different. Something within her directed Smriti to open the cards. To her surprise it was an invitation from the same host who by then had relocated himself and was placed in Mumbai. Smriti ran to Dinesh to inform him about the invitation. Her excitement baffled Dinesh as it was normally Smriti who always refused to go to such parties. "You will soon come to know the reason," was all that she informed Dinesh. "Do pick me up around 10 o'clock."

Sharp at 10 pm the door bell rang. Dinesh stood awestruck. He had never seen Smriti look so ravishing! She was in her low-back, red evening gown, her black hair cascading down to her slim sensuous waist. Dinesh could do nothing but hold her and give the tightest kiss. Any man would have been swayed and teased by such oozing sensuality. Smriti's face glowed with that kiss and she promised Dinesh something which he had been longing for.

Around 10.30 they stepped into the party. Smriti's presence did raise a hush, eyes got glued and wherever she moved she attracted a large number of guests. The ambience was exactly the same as a decade back. The party pulsating with loud music and dance, throbbing with esteemed guests from the corporate and glamour world, bureaucrats and celebrities, abounding in delicious food and overflowing with the most expensive wine, was the most sensational happening in the city that night. It was indeed a treat for the eyes.

Smriti moved around with Dinesh, her eyes hovering to find that single person who had brought so much pain and defamed her. Suddenly Smriti stopped and in split seconds she was not to be seen anymore by Dinesh. Smriti was just behind her prey waiting for her to turn. Losing patience she addressed and spoke to her, "If I am not mistaken, I think I know you, Maam", Smriti's heart ached as she spoke to her. Though she had changed a lot with hair turning grey with age and a few extra, unwanted pounds, yet Smriti could never forget that face. The lady left her group and proceeded to join Smriti. "Do I know you, young lady?" she enquired. Smriti lost her stability and yelled, "How could you forget me? You had sent me to jail for no reason, destroyed my career, defamed me just for a silly doubt. How could you do it?" saying this Smriti broke down. All eyes fell on the lady and out of shame she seeked forgiveness for what she had done years back. She revealed how she had victimized Smriti for her baseless doubt and how she had destroyed this young woman.

Dinesh came running from the other corner and taking Smriti in his bosom carried her back to their car. Dinesh had all the answers to his unanswered questions. He never questioned Smriti anything but just comforted her till they reached her home. Sriti cried like a child clinging onto Dinesh. Not a word was spoken as Dinesh wanted her to release all her pain that had welled up in her all these years. That was the only means to cleanse her of all the frustrations that had been in her, struggling so long to find release.

* * *

Chapter 11

"Would you mind staying back with me, tonight?" requested Smriti as their car came to a halt near her gate. Dinesh was aghast to hear this from her as he had never expected Smriti to be in such a miserable state. He didn't know what to say. Pretending not to hear what she had just said, he opened the car door for her. Smriti helplessly held his hand, "Please stay back, tonight." Dinesh had no other option but to give in to her desperate pleadings.

Smriti managed to regain her composure in her sweet home. Dinesh not anticipating what would follow next, waited for Smriti. Soon Smriti returned with two glasses and a bottle of white wine, they both enjoyed. "I want to celebrate tonight. I am eventually liberated." Dinesh got confused at her words yet never asked anything. He waited patiently for Smriti to reveal her past. Smriti poured the wine into the two glasses and offered one to Dinesh. Sipping her favourite drink she rested herself on Dinesh's chest. Tears rolled as she flipped through the pages of her past—her torturous experience in marriage, the traumatic incident in the train, her stay in Bangalore, her slander at the party, the torture and humiliation in the police custody and finally her seclusion. How she had combated every move of providence all by herself.

Dinesh had never seen this side of Smriti. Her tenderness touched him deeply. He sat up the whole night holding her in his bosom, caressing and comforting her. When the night had bid adieu they never realised. They had fallen asleep on the couch clinging onto each other.

The first ray of the morning sun kissed Smriti's cheeks to wake her up. She felt embarrassed as she found herself with Dinesh in a compromising position. As she tried to release herself from Dinesh's arms, he woke up and pulled her near him and kissed her forehead. Their eyes locked and their unspoken words spoke of their immense love. Dinesh could not take his eyes off her. Smriti still looked so angelic in spite of her flushed face that had resulted from the night long crying.

Her beauty was pure and refreshing and that captivating look in her eyes took his breath away. The image of Smriti in that red gown with her slender neck, sloping shoulders and sensuous cleavage swam before his eyes. Dinesh took her hand and brushed a kiss allowing his lips to have a lingering feel as his emotions were not entirely in control and he knew he would be unable to check himself. Smriti too was struggling with the same attraction as the most enticing smile crossed her visage. They decided to take a break and go for a long drive away from the maddening crowd.

The car moved aimlessly along the bay, out of the city, through the outskirts till it reached the countryside. Something urged them to stop at a place. There could not have been a more beautiful place than this—miles and miles of wild untamed acreage, fragrance of the wild flowers floating in the languid air, white puffy clouds nestling all over the sky, the whole ambience vibrated with a magical serenity. What a place to be in bliss with a beautiful companion! Soon their hearts pounded, desire pooled and unfurled everywhere. Their insatiable bodies wrapped in sensual caress moaned under the outburst. Dinesh planted a kiss on her forehead as he wrapped his arms around her once again.

* * *

Chapter 12

Back in office, Smriti was too preoccupied with the long list of POA lying on her table. The past two days she was completely out of touch. Her world was in utter doldrums. And now she had to catch a flight in two hours to Delhi for an assignment. Her flight tickets were kept on her desk. She was left with no time to go home and pack. For emergency, she always used to keep her travelling kit ready in the office, so decided to leave for the airport.

Smriti just needed to inform Dinesh to take care of her apartment. So she called him up on her way. "Please go and check out if everything is in order in my apartment," Smriti told Dinesh as he used to have the duplicate key to her house.

After work on his way back home, Dinesh dropped in at Smriti's place. He checked on everything—the gas cylinder, the electric points, gadgets and the locks. After ensuring that everything was fine, Dinesh wanted to sit for sometimes and have a drink as he felt terribly fatigued. He got a can of beer for himself from the fridge, lit a cigarette and relaxed in the couch.

The table in front of him was loaded with official papers and files. Dinesh scrutinized them. Suddenly his eyes caught onto a file which was quite a misfit there among the official papers. Curiosity aroused and he flipped through the pages of the file. It was Smriti's priceless possession which she denied to share with anyone. Her collection of poems, her feelings reflected on each leaf. Dinesh could not leave till he finished reading them. As he read through the lines his heart ached in feeling Smriti's pain. How beautifully had she transformed her pain into words! Dinesh was amazed at her talent. It should not go waste in any way. Dinesh had to do something about it. But what? Smriti would never share these on her own and he could not have asked her directly. Whatever was to be done had to be done discreetly.

He hurriedly finished his beer; he had only a day in hand before Smriti's return. So he took the file went back to office to make a copy of the collection. He suddenly remembered something—just six months! So without wasting any further time he called up one of his publisher friend. He willingly agreed to Dinesh's request. Dinesh was always very quick in his moves. He never liked to linger things and this needed quicker action.

Meanwhile Smriti was back from her tour. Her trip proved exceptionally profitable for both of them. Within the next six months the company saw impressive progress. Business contracts started flowing in. Sales swelled up. New business opportunities developed and their business touched the highest rung of success. This rapid growth spoke of the efficiency and confidence of the owners to cater and understand their clients.

* * *

Chapter 13

After a hectic day's work Smriti was relaxing at her home over a cup of coffee and music. That was the time she reveled in her own space and refused to entertain any intruder. But that day she was feeling a tad low as no one remembered it was her birthday. Even Dinesh did not wish her the whole day. The sudden ringing of the door bell disrupted her tranquility. Not very happy to welcome whoever it was, yet she was forced to attend the bell. It was Dinesh and she could not but welcome him. He was in real haste. "Get ready fast, we gotta attend an event," said Dinesh. Smriti tried to make pleas to avoid it but he would not agree. "Again official work!" Smriti sighed. She was sort of disgusted as the work load was pressing on her. Left with no option, Smriti dressed herself as quickly as possible. She looked gorgeous in her black tight skirt with a black jacket and high heels, her hair dropping till her waist. Dinesh was in awe looking at her.

It took them almost an hour to reach the venue due to the normal traffic problem in the city. Smriti was very inquisitive about the event because no prior invitation had come to her. She went on probing but Dinesh concentrated on his driving and the music. Soon the car reached the gates of Grand Hyatt. Dinesh held her hand and walked straight into the lounge. At the reception Smriti received an unusually warm welcome, not the usual decorum maintained in such 5 star hotels but something far more special. By then Smriti was sure that all those arrangements were Dinesh's special way of greeting her. But as they stepped into the conference hall where the event was happening, Smriti started feeling uncomfortable. All around the room were Smriti's pictures. Seeing the words on the backdrop on the dais Smriti was astounded. She failed to understand how exactly did all this happen and was caught between why and when. Dinesh ushered her to the front seat specially kept for her.

This was Smriti's dream come true ! The event was her own book launch that Dinesh and his friend had so discreetly organized. Smriti was completely baffled at the happening. The room abounded with celebrities and press personals. Smriti heard her bones rattling as she was ushered onto the dais for her book to be launched with all grandeur and honour. As a norm Sriti read out one of her poems that summed up the reason for her inspiration. Smriti was all in tears of joy with the appreciations and when she managed to regain her composure she confessed that this came as a bolt from the blue to her as she knew nothing how it happened. Standing awestruck in midst of the standing ovation she looked up to thank that force for all the gratification. Dinesh welcomed her with open arms as she stepped down from the dias.

Smriti could not help but hug him tightly in public for everything he did. "Happy Birthday, my love", Dinesh kissed to wish her.

Back home Smriti stood at her window overlooking the sea clasping her book in her hand, the most precious gift that Dinesh had just given her. Her dream transformed into reality, she rejoiced in the recollections of her victory.

However cruel and painful the sting of providence may be, one can still start afresh and win the strife. In life's journey there is nothing one cannot make if one sets one's heart to it. There are no mountains one may not climb, no deserts one may not cross, if resolute. Though time had endowed Smriti with sufficient agony, yet it was bound to bless her with immense gratification, maybe because of her defiance and strength to withstand the play of providence.

Thus evolved Smriti complete! Today her dreams are fulfilled, she is a celebrity with a successful career having a beautiful home and the love of her life, Dinesh. What more one could have asked from life?

* * *